Aurora
The Perfect Party

By Wendy Loggia
Illustrated by Studio IBOIX
and Gabriella Matta

DISNEY PRESS
Los Angeles • New York

Printed in China
First Box Set Edition, May 2017
1 3 5 7 9 10 8 6 4 2
FAC-025393-17142
ISBN 978-1-368-00879-2

For more Disney Press fun, visit www.disneybooks.com

Aurora

The Perfect Party

"Now the fun
really begins!"
——Aurora

Chapter One

$\mathcal{P}$rincess Aurora opened her violet eyes. Sunlight was streaming through her bedroom window. "Another beautiful day," she said with a smile, stretching her arms overhead. She had just had the most delightful dream. She dreamed that she was back living in the woodcutter's cottage with the three good fairies: Flora, Fauna, and Merryweather.

For sixteen years, Aurora had lived in the forest with the fairies. She didn't know she was a princess or that she was being hidden from the evil fairy Maleficent. The good fairies had named her Briar Rose. They pretended to be her aunts and gave her a wonderful, happy childhood.

Aurora was still adjusting to life in the palace after a year of being back in her real home. She hopped out of bed and walked over to the window. Her husband, Prince Phillip, was outside feeding his horse a carrot.

The princess pushed the window open. "Good morning!" she called, waving.

The prince turned. "Good morning, sleepyhead!" he said, looking up with a smile. "I'm just about to take Samson for a ride. Would you like to join me?"

Aurora thought for a minute. It would be fun to go for a morning horseback ride with

Phillip. But her dream had made her eager to see the fairies.

"Maybe next time!" she said. "Have fun!"

The prince waved. Then he climbed on Samson and trotted off.

Aurora stepped into her closet and looked through a rack of beautiful gowns in all the colors of the rainbow.

"Princess Aurora?" One of the palace servants knocked softly on her bedroom door. "The cook has made some delicious blueberry pancakes for you. Of course, there are also scrambled eggs, if you'd rather have those. Or a big bowl of strawberries and whipped cream might suit?"

Aurora laughed. "Oh, the cook is too kind. I certainly won't go hungry," she said.

"I'll be down in just a moment." Aurora reached for a long, flowing pink gown and her favorite pair of shoes. She dressed quickly and hurried down the hallway.

The castle was the biggest, most beautiful place Aurora had ever seen. It seemed each stairway and each closed door led to a new room. She still hadn't had the chance to see everything!

"Hello! Good morning." Aurora greeted the servants who were bustling to and fro. There was a cooking staff and a cleaning staff and a gardening staff. There was even a staff to polish the royal jewels! It took a lot of people to keep the castle in tip-top shape.

"You look pretty as a daisy!" Flora said. She floated down the hallway toward Aurora

with Fauna and Merryweather at her side.

When Aurora and Phillip had gotten married, the three fairies had moved into the castle, too. They had an entire wing just to themselves.

"Why, thank you." Aurora smiled and twirled around. "Can you join me for breakfast?"

"Let's check our calendar," Fauna said. She pulled out her magic wand and *poof!* a calendar hovered in the air in front of them.

"It looks like we're available," Flora said. Fauna was just about to zap the calendar away when Merryweather stopped her.

"Wait just a minute! Do you realize what's coming up?" She looked at Fauna's, Flora's, and Aurora's puzzled faces. "It's almost one year ago today that we all moved into the castle together!"

"A whole year," Fauna said, sighing happily.

"My, how time flies," said Flora, shaking her head. "It seems like only yesterday we were living in the woodcutter's cottage."

"I dreamed about the cottage last night!" Aurora exclaimed. "You all took such good care of me there. I can never thank you enough for all you did."

"We loved every minute of it, my dear," Merryweather replied.

"Every second," Fauna added.

"Every . . . every . . . every moment," Flora declared. "Sometimes I wish we could all go back there to live together again."

The fairies chattered on about their favorite memories from the cottage as they entered the royal dining room with Aurora. Suddenly, the princess had an idea.

I'm going to throw the fairies a grand surprise party to celebrate our first year together in the castle, she thought with excitement. The princess knew the palace staff would be busy planning her birthday party, which was just over a week away. But she would throw the surprise party for the fairies a couple of days before. It would be the biggest, grandest celebration the castle had ever seen!

Chapter Two

After breakfast, the fairies went off on their own, giving Aurora time to plan. She went to her bedroom and pulled a pink journal and a plumed blue pen from her desk. "Now, what kind of party would they like best?" she said aloud, tapping her chin.

Outside the door, she heard the fairies'

voices. Aurora walked quietly down the hall, and the sounds grew louder. Flora, Fauna, and Merryweather were outside on one of the castle terraces.

Tiptoeing close to the large glass doors that opened onto the terrace, Aurora ducked behind a long velvet drape. She held her journal tightly.

"Ahh, yes. That looks just splendid," Fauna said. She was arranging a gigantic bouquet of flowers in a crystal vase. The vase hovered in the air. The fairies didn't like to do anything without magic! Fauna snipped off a few leaves and adjusted some petals. Then she stepped back to look at her creation. "If only I had some forget-me-nots."

"Are those the pink and blue flowers you used to pick?" Flora asked from the other side of the terrace. She was flitting around, monitoring the watering cans she'd enchanted as they swooped over the flowerpots, pouring just the right amount of water into them.

"Yes. They're my absolute favorite," Fauna replied.

"You know, you could always turn those roses into forget-me-nots," Merryweather said, eyeing Fauna's wand. The blue fairy was busy untangling the strings of some wind chimes.

Fauna sighed. "That's not the same. They never smell as fragrant. The best ones in the whole world grow in a flower bed near the

woodcutter's cottage." She shook her head. "There are some things that even magic can't do."

Smiling to herself, Aurora opened her journal and wrote:

Forget-me-nots
(pink and blue)
for Fauna.

Then she listened some more.

"I do know what you mean, Fauna," Merryweather said. "I love my bedroom here at the castle, of course. It couldn't be any nicer! But there was a group of songbirds who had a nest near my room in the cottage. Waking up to that concert every morning was one of my favorite things. I miss it terribly."

Aurora wrote in her book again:

A chorus of songbirds for Merryweather.

"And while we're at it, let's not forget all the sweet red strawberries Briar Rose—I mean, Aurora—used to gather on her walks," Flora said, nodding. "They were so juicy and delicious!"

Aurora wrote a third note:

Strawberries for Flora.
Must be delicious!

The princess looked over her list. *That's it!* she thought. *We'll have a grand party made up of the simple things we all miss from our time in the forest.* She smiled, delighted with her idea.

Aurora turned and walked back down the hallway before the fairies discovered her.

She paused outside the royal ballroom. This was one of her favorite places in the castle. She and Phillip had held several parties there for their friends.

Aurora stepped inside the empty ballroom. Heavy crystal chandeliers hung from the ceiling, and mirrors, and tapestries lined the walls. She looked down at her notebook. Flowers, birds, and strawberries. It was funny how the simplest of things could make the fairies happy. She could just imagine how the elegant room would look with a chorus of songbirds and vases filled with forget-me-nots. This party would certainly be a change from what the palace staff was used to.

"Aurora? Is that you?" Prince Phillip poked his head inside the ballroom's grand doorway. "What are you doing in here all by yourself?"

"Planning the most perfect party in the world!" she exclaimed. She ran over and gave the prince a hug, laughing as he twirled her around. The princess told Phillip about her idea. "Won't it be a wonderful surprise for the fairies?"

Phillip scratched his head. "Strawberries and birds?" he asked. "That sounds so . . . well, it sounds lovely."

Aurora smiled. "I knew you would agree!" she said. "I'm going to need your help," she continued.

The prince got down on one knee and waved his arm with a royal flourish. "At your service, milady. Your wish is my command."

Aurora giggled. "Then, please darling, stand up. We haven't got a moment to waste!"

Chapter Three

"What do you think of this one?" Aurora asked. She had a floppy orange hat on her head. Then she pulled it off and put on a straw hat with long pink ribbons that tied under her chin. "Or is this better?"

Aurora and Phillip were upstairs in the castle. Aurora was trying on hats and wigs

while the prince sat on a cushioned bench watching her. He looked very bored and a little confused. "I'm still trying to figure out what exactly is going on," he said.

The princess took a deep breath. "This party has to remain a secret. It will be unlike any event the fairies or the castle has ever seen."

"There have been a lot of events here," the prince reminded her. "We've had every theme imaginable—masked balls, holiday dances, birthday teas . . ."

Aurora's eyes were shining. "I know! That's exactly my point. This will be a completely different kind of party. Something that will remind the fairies of the time when we all lived together in the forest." She gave Phillip a kiss on the cheek. "The fairies are so dear, and they've done so much for me and my family. But we did have such fun when I was a little girl." She remembered blowing bubbles as they did the dishes and

dancing with a broom when it was time to clean.

Phillip smiled. "I think it's the sweetest of ideas, Aurora. But what do all the hats and wigs have to do with the party?"

Laughing, Aurora reached up and put a velvet blue bonnet on her head. "In order to make this party perfect, I'm going to have to go back to the cottage to collect these items. They all have meaning for the fairies. And I can't go out into the woods wearing my royal gown and tiara. If I do, someone will recognize me, and word could get back to the fairies. I need to wear a disguise."

Philip thought for a minute. "Can one of the servants go instead?"

The princess had considered that. But everyone was busy planning for *her* birthday party. She wanted to do as much of the work for this party as she possibly could. "I know right where the flowers are. And the strawberries. Plus, I really want this to be a gift from me."

"Well, what if I go with you?" Phillip suggested.

But Aurora shook her head. "It will take some time to gather everything," she said. "If we're both gone for that long, the fairies will suspect something."

The prince nodded. "I'll keep the fairies distracted. Do you think you can finish in time?"

Aurora bit her lip. "I hope so. The

party will be held four days from now. I'll have three days to find what I need, and on the last day we can decorate.

"Now," she said, turning back to the pile of hats, "it's time to find something completely unprincesslike!"

Chapter Four

$\mathcal{L}$ater that day, while the fairies were taking their afternoon nap, Aurora snuck out of the castle. She looked down at her simple lavender and white dress. She had decided on a white hat with a purple bow, and her long blond hair was tucked up under it. On her arm, she carried an empty woven basket to fill with flowers and berries.

Aurora smiled as she hurried away from the castle. She thought she looked just like any other subject in the kingdom. She was sure no one would recognize her. With a small skip in her step, she turned down a narrow wooded path that was lined on either side with tall trees and ferns.

The woodcutter's cottage was a fair distance from the castle. After walking for some time, Aurora stepped into a sunny clearing and sighed with happiness. "The cottage!" she exclaimed.

Her old home looked just as she remembered it—the thatched roof, the small windows, the winding walk that led to the front door. It did seem a little smaller

now that she had grown used to living in a castle. But the charming little cottage was every bit as dear and welcoming to her as it had always been.

Joyfully, Aurora began to sing. Within

a few moments, her voice had drawn some woodland animals.

"Why, you recognize me, don't you?" she said, as two chirping bluebirds landed on a nearby tree branch.

Two fluffy-tailed squirrels stood holding acorns. Three small chipmunks had stopped chasing each other to listen to her sing. And a group of cottontail rabbits gathered at her feet.

"I've missed you all so much," the princess said, smiling at her old friends.

Suddenly, the sound of approaching hoofbeats startled Aurora. Someone was coming!

"Oh!" Aurora cried with a gasp. She hastily adjusted her hat.

A cart came into view, carrying a farmer and his family. They pulled to a stop beside the cottage.

"Good day, madame," the farmer said as he tipped his hat to Aurora. "Do you happen to know which road leads back to the village? We seem to have taken a wrong turn somewhere."

Aurora smiled. She gave the farmer directions. "When you see the castle turrets over the hill, you'll know you're almost there," she said.

"Thank you, dear," the farmer's wife said. "We've been going in circles for an hour! You've been so kind to help. Won't you please take some berries?"

Aurora kindly accepted a basket of

plump blackberries. "Thank you," she said and popped a berry into her mouth. "Mmm, these are delicious!"

The farmer and his wife thanked Aurora again. Then they set off on their way.

Aurora turned back to her animal friends. "Well, clearly my disguise worked!" she exclaimed.

The princess told the animals all about the surprise party she was planning for the fairies. "Will you help me? You're all invited to the big event, of course."

The animals chirped, chattered, and hopped. "I'll take that as a yes!" Aurora said happily.

A shadow passed overhead, and the princess looked up at the sky. The sun was starting to set. "My goodness! I must be on my way!" If she didn't leave now, it would be dark by the time she returned to the castle. "And I haven't even crossed one item off my party list!" she said, sighing. "Oh, well. At least the guests have been invited!"

Chapter Five

Fauna, Flora, and Merryweather were pacing in the main hall of the castle. When they saw Aurora coming down the staircase, they fluttered to her side. She'd snuck back into the castle and quickly changed into her pink gown.

"Princess Aurora! Where have you

been?" Fauna asked. "We woke up and you were gone!"

"We were beginning to worry about you," Flora said, throwing her arms around the princess in a tight hug.

Merryweather nodded. "We woke up from our naps, and the prince told us you were in the stables. When we couldn't find you there, he said you might be in the kitchen. Then he thought that perhaps you'd gone for a walk in the garden."

Just then, Prince Phillip walked into the room. "Ah, you've found her! I should have thought to check the main hall."

Aurora tried not to laugh. The prince was doing a great job of distracting the fairies. She couldn't wait to tell him how well her disguise had worked. Planning a surprise party was turning out to be a lot of fun!

The next morning, Aurora put on another simple dress, this one blue. She tied her long blond hair back with a scarf.

"Remember, you must keep the fairies distracted again," she told the prince. They were behind the royal stables, hiding from the palace attendants.

"I've got it all covered," he said. "Last night, I told the fairies how much I loved that cake they made for my birthday and asked if they could make it again today."

Aurora frowned. "But that won't take them long at all!"

"It will if they can't find their wands," the prince said. He pulled three wands from his scabbard.

"That's absolutely . . . perfect!" Aurora exclaimed. The fairies would be shocked when they woke up to find their wands missing. For a moment she felt bad about upsetting them. But then she thought about the party she had planned for them. It would all be worth it.

The prince kissed her cheek. "Now, go!"

When Aurora arrived at the cottage, she set off down a worn footpath that led to Fauna's favorite flower bed. It wasn't far from the cottage's front door. She carried a basket in the crook of her arm.

The sweet smell of the flowers told Aurora she was almost there. "Fauna was right," she said as she came to a large bed of pink and blue forget-me-nots. "Not even magic could create something as beautiful as this!"

She knelt down and took out the pair of garden shears she carried in her basket. Then she began to carefully cut enough flowers to make one of the biggest bouquets Fauna had ever seen.

When Aurora was finished, she hurried back to the castle. She quickly hid the basket of flowers behind one of the long drapes in her room.

Aurora took out her pink journal and put a big check mark next to:

✓ Forget-me-nots
(pink and blue)
for Fauna.

Then she changed into another gown and went downstairs.

The fairies were in the kitchen. Fauna was mixing something in a bowl. She had frosting on her hat. Flora's cheeks had some bright pink icing on them. She'd turned pink. And Merryweather had dough on her face.

"My, my, it smells delicious in here," Aurora said. "What's the occasion?"

"The prince asked us to make him a special cake," Fauna explained.

"And you decided not to use magic. How wonderful!" Aurora said. She dipped her finger in the frosting for a taste.

"Yes, well, we, um, decided it would be more special that way," Merryweather said

as Flora backed her up with an anxious nod.

"I'm sure he'll appreciate it so much," Aurora told them. Then she left the fairies to their baking. Her plan was working out perfectly!

Chapter Six

*L*ater that night, Aurora found Prince Phillip tiptoeing out of the fairies' wing of the castle.

"I put their wands on Merryweather's bookshelf," the prince whispered. "I'm afraid they were worried about losing them."

Aurora felt terrible. "The poor dears."

But she was almost done planning the party! And the fairies still had no idea she'd been sneaking out of the palace.

She had set off on another trip that morning. She wore a straw hat and a bright red dress that she thought was the same color as the strawberries she was looking for.

Along the way, Aurora took a wrong turn. The sun was high in the sky when she realized her mistake and had to double back. She was very tired, and a little frustrated. But the thought of Flora's delight over the most delicious strawberries in the forest made her to keep going.

When at last she had found the old spot, she discovered that the berries weren't ripe enough yet. "Oh, no!" she cried. "What am I going to bring Flora now?"

Suddenly, a robin flew over and landed on Aurora's shoulder. She quickly explained what she was looking for: "The sweetest strawberries ever to be had!" The robin tweeted and flew further down the path. Aurora hurried to keep up. When at last the robin stopped, Aurora clapped with delight. "Oh, thank you!" she said as she looked at row after row of bright red wild strawberries.

She popped one of the strawberries into her mouth. "Delicious!" she said. "These are exactly what Flora is looking for."

Aurora filled her basket to the top. Then she pulled out her journal and looked at the note.

"I think I've found the yummiest berries in the kingdom!" she exclaimed, checking it off.

✓ Strawberries for Flora.
Must be delicious!

"Now just one more thing," she said. The robin was still chirping sweetly.

The robin couldn't help her pick berries. But he could help Aurora with a different task. She described her last item, and the robin flew off. He returned a few minutes later with a bluebird and some other friends. Tweeting and singing, the birds made the most wonderful chorus Aurora had ever heard.

"You must come tomorrow night and sing

for Merryweather," she said. "Please, say you will."

The birds tweeted happily.

"Oh, thank you," Aurora said. "You've done so much for me already. Do you think you could do one more thing?"

The birds chirped.

"Wonderful." She leaned forward and said, "Could you deliver a message to the castle for me?"

The birds chirped louder.

"Thank you all so much!" Aurora said. She carefully tore a piece of paper from her journal and wrote a note. Then she folded it in half and handed it to the robin. "Please make sure this goes to Claude, the butler."

The robin flew off with the scrap of paper tucked firmly in his beak.

Aurora looked at the last item on her list. She smiled as she placed a third and final check beside it.

✓ A chorus of songbirds
for Merryweather.

Chapter Seven

$\mathcal{B}$ack at the castle, Aurora spread a linen napkin over the basket of strawberries. Then she pushed it into the back of the pantry, where it was cool.

"There," Aurora said. She knew that after baking a cake without wands, the fairies were unlikely to return soon. They would never see the strawberries in the pantry.

The biggest delivery of party supplies was yet to come. Aurora had arranged for the items to be hidden in the stables until the next morning. Everything had all come together perfectly!

Aurora changed out of her red dress and put on a pretty purple gown. She ran downstairs and out onto the back lawn, where she spotted a green blur, a blue blur, and a red blur. The three fairies were on their hands and knees searching through the grass. "Flora? Fauna? Merryweather? What's going on?"

"Oh, Princess, hello!" Flora said, jumping up. Her skirt was covered in clover, and her cheeks were as pink as her dress.

"Prince Phillip had the most terrible luck. He—"

"He lost a rare jewel this morning!" Fauna interrupted. "It fell out of his pocket while he was riding Samson! We've been looking for it for hours."

"Oh, my goodness," Aurora exclaimed. *Phillip must be frantic*, Aurora thought. Then she spotted him walking across the lawn toward them.

"Phillip! I just heard what happened," she said, running to him. To her surprise, he gave her a wink. Ahhh, she realized. This is another distraction for the fairies!

"And wouldn't you know, the jewel has a spell on it. It can't be found by magic," Merryweather said huffily.

The prince held out his hand. Sitting in his palm was a glittering emerald-colored gem. "It turns out I didn't drop it after all," he told them, wearing a sheepish grin. "It was in my pocket all along."

"In your pocket all along?" Flora repeated wearily.

"Isn't that wonderful," Fauna said, yawning. Her hat had slid down to one side of her head, but she smiled.

Merryweather grunted. "Next time perhaps Your Highness might check his pockets more thoroughly before sending us on a wild-goose chase."

"Merryweather!" Fauna whispered, giving the fairy a nudge.

But Phillip nodded. "I don't blame

Merryweather for feeling frustrated. And I'm so sorry to have troubled you. Why don't you go inside and rest?"

Aurora agreed. "I'll have the cook make you your favorite dinner."

"That sounds lovely," Flora said gratefully. The fairies flew slowly back to the castle.

"Keeping the party a secret hasn't been easy," Prince Phillip told Aurora as soon as the fairies were out of earshot.

"Only one more time to distract the dears—tomorrow morning," Aurora told him happily. "I need to make sure they're far away from the royal ballroom so we can set everything up for their party." She reached for his hand, and they walked toward the castle. "Now the fun really begins!"

Chapter Eight

"Hmmm, let's see. How about there?" Aurora pointed across the ballroom. "Right underneath that big crystal chandelier."

"As you wish, Your Highness," a palace servant said. He and another servant moved the dining table from the woodcutter's cottage to the center of the room. It looked small and rustic in the elegant ballroom. Aurora beamed with pride as more servants carried in the cottage's chairs and another group balanced the cottage's dishes on large silver trays. The day of the party had finally arrived. And now, her vision for the grandest celebration the castle had ever seen was coming to life!

The message she'd given to the birds in the forest was for a carriage to be sent to the cottage. The servants had loaded the dining furniture and other items onto it and snuck them into the castle.

"That's where our guests of honor will sit," Aurora told the servants as they arranged the chairs.

She picked up a familiar pink teacup

and smiled. She knew the fairies would be thrilled to see these items from their old life.

Aurora snuck back to her room for the basket of wildflowers. When she got back to the ballroom, the princess supervised as workers decorated columns with intertwining ivy garlands. Then she helped make sure that beautiful vases of forget-me-nots were placed throughout the room.

Claude, the butler, hurried over to talk with Aurora. He was very eager to make sure the day was perfect. "Is everything as you wish, Princess?"

"Oh, yes," Aurora told him, her eyes shining. "The fairies will love it."

"We even found a band of local musicians to play for us," Claude said. He pointed to

the band members, who were setting up their instruments.

"Wonderful! The fairies love to sing and dance," Aurora told him. Then she giggled as she watched the palace staff place simple tablecloths and hand-painted wooden candlesticks on the tables. They were definitely different table settings than the royal family and their guests were used to!

A young woman, new to the palace staff, shyly came over to Aurora. "Your Highness?" She gave a low curtsy. "I found this in the upstairs hall. I believe it is yours?"

Aurora's eyes widened as the servant handed her the journal. All her notes for the party were in there!

"Oh, dear me," she said. "I must have dropped it on my way to breakfast this morning. I don't know what I would have done if the fairies had stumbled upon it. Our party could have been ruined!" She gave the young woman a grateful smile. "Thank you so very much."

Aurora clutched the journal to her chest. *What if the fairies saw it?* she thought. Was her surprise spoiled? She took a deep breath. The only thing to do was to keep preparing for the party.

Claude suddenly started waving his hands in the air, trying to get everyone's attention. "*S'il vous plaît!* Quiet, everyone! Shhh! I just received word that the fairies are coming down the hallway right now. We

must be quiet as mice. We don't want them to know we're in here."

A hush fell over the grand ballroom, and Aurora's heart leaped into her throat. The fairies couldn't walk in now. The royal party guests hadn't even arrived yet! After all the hard work she, Prince Phillip, and the palace staff had done, was the surprise about to be spoiled?

Chapter Nine

Everyone in the royal ballroom stopped what they were doing. Aurora's heart was racing. All her planning, all the flowers and strawberries and the songbird concert . . . the surprise couldn't be ruined now. After what seemed like forever she heard a loud voice from behind the oak doors.

"Flora, Fauna, Merryweather! Please, wait!"

Aurora gasped. It was Prince Phillip!

"Yes, Your Highness?" the fairies said. "How can we help you?"

"There's a frog in the back garden who says you enchanted him. He's quite unhappy and he, uh, he wants to return to normal."

"I haven't enchanted any frogs lately," Fauna said. "Have you, Merryweather?"

"Not all month," the fairy replied.

There was a loud sigh from Flora. "I did turn a pesky rabbit into a frog last week. He just wouldn't stop eating my lilies, and I couldn't stand it any longer. It served him right. It did."

The prince cleared his throat. "Well, the

frog that was once a rabbit is asking to be
turned back to his normal state. He seems
rather finicky. Please, come see him?"

It seemed that everyone in the ballroom was holding their breath as they waited to hear the fairies' reply.

A moment later Aurora and the staff heard the fairies' shoes clicking along the hallway floor.

They were going to see the frog.

The servants exchanged relieved glances and got back to work. The party would still be a surprise after all!

Aurora checked the clock. It was almost time for the guests to arrive. She tiptoed upstairs to her room to get dressed for the party.

She pulled her favorite pink gown out of the closet. She'd thought for a moment about wearing one of her simple peasant dresses to the party. But she'd settled on the traditional gown instead. There would be plenty of royal guests as well as her forest friends.

After giving her long blond hair a quick brushing, Aurora hurried back to the ballroom. Guests from far and wide were beginning to arrive. Aurora hugged her parents and Phillip's father, King Hubert.

"What a fine party this is going to be," King Stefan said proudly as servants carried tray after tray of pies, frosted cakes, and iced cookies into the ballroom. He kissed his daughter's head. "Lovely job, my dear."

The queen nodded. "Yes, darling. What a perfect party! I couldn't think of anyone more deserving than our dear fairies."

Aurora tried to stay calm. She walked over to the doorway to greet the guests as they arrived. "Hello," Aurora said to a group of elegant ladies. "I'm so pleased you could be here." They looked beautiful in their gowns and jewels.

Then she heard some very nonroyal sounds.

Squawk.

Chip-chip-chip.

Tweet.

"You're here!" Aurora cried. Her friends from the woods—the bluebirds, cardinals, rabbits, chipmunks, squirrels, and owl— came into the ballroom. She looked kindly at the birds. "You know what to do, right?"

They tweeted back.

Aurora clasped her hands together. "Perfect."

Then Claude hurried over to her. "It's time, Princess. Are you ready?"

Aurora drew in a big breath. "I'm ready."

The room hushed. The lights dimmed. And then the heavy oak doors swung open.

The fairies came fluttering into the ballroom in the middle of a conversation.

"I should have left him as a frog," Flora was saying. "He was such a pushy fellow—"

"Surprise!" cried all the guests, rising to their feet and clapping loudly.

The fairies stopped. Their mouths dropped open.

Aurora gave the signal, and in an instant, all the candles in the room lit up. The windows swung open, letting in the summer breeze. And the birds began singing the sweetest song in the world.

"Surprise, my dears!" Aurora cried happily. "Surprise, surprise!"

Chapter Ten

"I still can't believe you planned all of this for us," Merryweather said, shaking her head. She gazed around the room. "The decorations, the food, the guests—why, it's all so amazing!"

"We didn't suspect a thing, dearie!" Fauna said merrily.

"This is the biggest surprise of our lives," Flora added.

Princess Aurora was sitting at the fairies' table in the center of the ballroom. The party was in full swing. The fairies had been shown to their special seats as the band struck up a tune. Servants brought the fairies all sorts of treats served on their old cottage dishes.

Fauna pressed her face into the bouquet on the table and inhaled deeply. "These are the sweetest-smelling forget-me-nots I've ever sniffed," she said.

"And the strawberries are just as I remember them," Flora said, dipping a big red one into a bowl of whipped cream. "No, wait. They're better!"

The songbirds finished serenading a delighted Merryweather. The fairy wagged a finger at the princess. "Very tricky you were, sending us on all those wild-goose chases."

Aurora gave an innocent shrug. "If I hadn't, I would never have been able to give you the party you deserve. But I can't take all the credit," Aurora said as Prince Phillip walked over to their table. "I didn't know my husband was so good at keeping secrets!"

The prince winked at the fairies. "I'm so sorry I had to distract you so. Will you forgive me?"

The fairies exchanged glances. At first they looked serious . . . but then they broke into happy smiles. "We do!" they said in unison.

"Then I hope you will honor me with a dance," he said, extending his hand to Fauna.

"Ooh! I'd love to," Fauna said. She took the prince's arm. As the band struck up their next song, Phillip and Fauna began to dance.

"My, but he's handsome," Flora said dreamily, leaning her chin on her hand. "Oops!" Her elbow knocked into her glass of fruit punch, toppling it over on the tablecloth. "Fiddlesticks," she said, dabbing the mess with some napkins.

"Here you go," Merryweather said, pulling out her wand. She zapped the tablecloth dry,

changing it to blue in the process.

"Thank you," Flora said. She pulled out her own wand. *Zap!* The tablecloth was purple.

"Oh, you dears," Aurora said, laughing. "Don't you know you aren't supposed to lift a wand at your own party?" She looked at them, her eyes dancing. "But I do think yellow would look absolutely perfect."

Zap! Suddenly the tablecloth was yellow. A startled Flora, Merryweather, and Aurora looked up to see Fauna waving her wand. "There we go!" she said breathlessly, tucking the wand back in her pocket. "Yellow it is." She plopped into a chair next to the princess and picked up her teacup. "I haven't danced like that in ages!"

"And I can see you haven't lost your touch," Aurora told her, patting her shoulder.

Just then, Prince Phillip came over to the table and bowed. "I've come to request the pleasure of another dance partner. Aurora, will you dance with me?"

Aurora turned to the fairies. "You don't mind, do you? Just for one dance?"

The fairies shook their heads. "Of course not," Merryweather replied. "Besides, it will give us some time to plan."

"Plan? Why, what do you mean?" Aurora asked, curious.

The fairies smiled. "Why, your birthday party, of course!" Flora said. "Only a few more days . . ."

The fairies winked. Aurora knew they

would do something special. Just as she had for them.

"Now, shoo!" Merryweather said, waving the couple off. "We've got things to discuss."

Laughing, the prince and princess waltzed onto the dance floor as Flora, Fauna, Merryweather, and the rest of the guests clapped to the beat. A pair of rabbits danced beside them as the owl swooped overhead.

"This has been the best year of my life!" Princess Aurora said happily. "I can't wait to see what happens next!"